MW00800615

For our Michael,
forever remembered,
forever loved

Kermit the Newf and Fozzie Bear
dedicate this book to all of the very special
children in their lives

MW00800615

www.mascotbooks.com

The Adventures of Kermit the Newf: Kermit Gets a Puppy

Story ©2019 Molly Tischler and Bonnie Giacovelli. All Rights Reserved.
No part of this publication may be reproduced, stored in a retrieval
system or transmitted in any form by any means electronic, mechanical, or
photocopying, recording or otherwise without the permission of the author.

Project Newf, LLC
For more information, visit www.KermitTheNewf.com

Illustrations ©2019 Amy Bolin

For more information, please contact:
Mascot Books
620 Herndon Parkway #320
Herndon, VA 20170
info@mascotbooks.com

Library of Congress Control Number: 2018912417

CPSIA Code: PBANG0119A
ISBN: 978-1-64307-301-9

Printed in the United States

THE ADVENTURES OF KERMIT THE NEWF

BOOK 2
KERMIT GETS A PUPPY

written by

Molly Tischler and Bonnie Giacovelli

illustrated by

Amy Bolin

As Kermit was napping by the dining room table he heard lots of walking around: up the stairs, down the stairs, out the front door, back in the house again.

I wonder what's going on, he thought. He opened
one eye and saw boxes, backpacks, and a cooler
full of food. He was too excited to go back to sleep
so he sat up and watched his owners Bonnie and
Lenny scurrying around the house.

Just as it seemed like they were finished, Grandma and Grandpa drove up. *Ah!* thought Kermit. *They must be going too. We're all going to have an adventure.* They all got into Grandma's big minivan and settled in for what turned out to be a very long ride.

After four hours in the van, they arrived at their friend's house in the middle of the state of Florida. She had a large house with 20 acres of land, a huge pond, and 15 Newfoundland dogs. *Yay! Hooray!* Kermit knew exactly where he was. This was the house where he was born. He knew all the dogs that lived there. Some of them were even his sisters and brothers. He was so excited he could hardly wait until they opened the van door to let him out.

Kermit ran all around the house looking for his friends. His crazy tail wagged in every direction. When his friends saw him, they all got just as excited as Kermit. The sounds of happy barking could be heard for miles. What a great SURPRISE this was. However, the SURPRISES were just beginning.

Kermit next went to the fenced area of the yard. There he saw two adorable, ten-week-old puppies standing next to his sister Willow. They were tiny black and white fur balls.

Bonnie, Lenny, Grandma, and Grandpa came into the fenced yard too. Bonnie pointed to the puppies and said, "Kermit, those little ones are Willow's puppies. That means they're your niece and nephew."

Wow! thought Kermit. *I'm an uncle!*

Kermit watched as the little girl puppy led the little boy puppy into a very dirty area of the yard. *I wonder what they are going to do*, thought Kermit.

Kermit followed them and watched as the little boy puppy started digging in the dirt. He was making a big hole! After he dug it deep enough, he laid down in it, curled up in a ball, and went to sleep.

That looks like fun, thought Kermit. *I think I'll do that too.*
Kermit dug and dug and flung dirt all over the yard.

When Kermit was done digging, he looked for the little boy puppy. *Oh no*, thought Kermit. *He's gone!* Just then he saw the tiniest motion in the dirt and a little paw appeared, followed by a little tail and a little head.

Then the little puppy stood up and shook himself off. Everyone laughed at the silly sight. "Time for a quick bath and brushing for you two," said Bonnie. "We can't let you in the van looking like that."

Kermit loved the bath and brushing but his little nephew wasn't so sure.

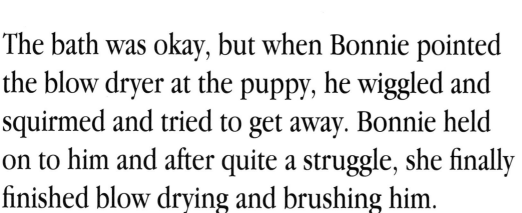

The bath was okay, but when Bonnie pointed the blow dryer at the puppy, he wiggled and squirmed and tried to get away. Bonnie held on to him and after quite a struggle, she finally finished blow drying and brushing him.

He looked so cute and fluffy, and he really felt better too.

Then the biggest surprise of the day came when Bonnie said to Kermit, "We will be taking your nephew home with us. He is your new puppy."

Wow, thought Kermit. *I will have a puppy of my very own. We can play together all the time. That will be so much fun.*

"What should we name him?" asked Bonnie. "The name has to be something special because this is a very special little puppy." After much deliberation, they came up with the name Fozzie Bear. After all, Fozzie Bear was going to be Kermit's new best friend.

Kermit and Fozzie Bear cuddled up in the back of the van and spent the long four hour ride home enjoying each other's company. On the way home, they stopped at a rest area to let the dogs stretch their legs and get some water. It was noisy and busy there and Fozzie Bear was frightened. He had never been to a place like this before.

Kermit walked up to Fozzie Bear and gave
him a quick nuzzle and let him know that he
was safe. Fozzie Bear felt a bit better and decided to
follow his Uncle Kermit. As long as he had Bonnie,
Lenny, and Kermit with him, he decided he would
be safe enough to walk around and get a drink. Then
it was back in the van to continue the
journey home.

The next day, they were out in the yard enjoying the beautiful Florida sunshine when a little girl named Jenna came over to say hello. Of course, she knew Kermit, but she was surprised to see Kermit with his very own puppy.

"Oh boy," she said. "You have a new puppy and I have a new baby sister. She is very small, but I can't wait till she gets bigger and we can play together."

As time went by, Fozzie Bear required more and more attention from Bonnie. He had to be walked very often because he was fed very often. He needed lots of brushing and, most of all, he needed lots of cuddling. Kermit started to become a bit jealous. He didn't eat as often or need to go out as often, but he certainly did need lots of cuddling.

Kermit also realized that Fozzie Bear was hiding his favorite toys under the bed. Kermit was too big to fit under there! Before long, Fozzie Bear had a huge stash of Kermit's toys hidden away.

The other thing that bothered Kermit was that every time he stood up to walk somewhere, Fozzie Bear jumped on his back. Being a very energetic puppy, Fozzie Bear always wanted to play and wrestle. Kermit, who was much older and calmer, didn't mind playing occasionally, but not every minute of every day. That was way too much for any big dog!

At the same time in the house down the street, Jenna
was having a similar problem with her baby sister Lisa.
Lisa had lots of energy and crawled all over the house.
She took Jenna's toys and hid them under the bed,
where Jenna couldn't reach them.

She also required a lot of her mother's attention because she had to be fed, bathed, changed and rocked to sleep. Jenna was feeling very left out because she was old enough to do most things for herself, but still young enough to want her mother's attention.

Bonnie was in the yard one day
and she overheard Jenna
telling Kermit how
unfair she was
being treated
and how much
time her mother was
spending with the baby
and not with her anymore.

Kermit listened very intently. He
understood what Jenna was saying because
he felt the same way about his new puppy. They both
loved their new babies, but it was often hard to share.

This gave Bonnie an idea!
She called Jenna's mother
and told her the plan.
"What a wonderful idea,"
she said. "Let's
do it."

The following day, Kermit and Jenna had the biggest surprise: they were going to a beach that allowed dogs! Pails, shovels, beach toys, and bumpers were packed, along with food and water. Kermit and Jenna couldn't wait!

When they got to the beach, Jenna's mom laid out a blanket and put their food and toys on it. She then took Jenna into the ocean for a swim.

Bonnie threw Kermit's large orange bumper way out into the water. Kermit swam out to retrieve it and brought it back to her. They all enjoyed playing in the water. When they finished swimming, Kermit shook the water off him and got them all wet again.

Before long, it was time for lunch and a drink of water, then it was back to playing again. First Kermit and Jenna dug a big hole in the sand. Jenna laid down in it and Kermit turned his back to her and proceeded to throw sand on her with his front legs.

When she was completely covered except for her face, he went over and licked her face, wagged his crazy tail, and then sat down on top of her belly.

This made her laugh so hard that her belly shook and Kermit bounced up and down. Kermit loved it. He felt like he was on a ride in an amusement park!

Jenna started digging her way out and pushed Kermit off with one big shove. Kermit helped her dig the rest of the way out.

Then she started digging a hole and this time, Kermit got in it and laid down on his belly and curled up ready for a nap, but that was not going to happen.

Jenna filled her pail with sand and poured it all over Kermit. She kept doing it until he was almost completely covered. Then she laid down on top of him and pretended to go to sleep too. That was fun for a while, but Kermit got too hot, so he wiggled and wriggled his way out from under the sand and threw Jenna off him. She laughed again and followed him into the cool ocean.

Kermit started swimming around in circles just waiting for Jenna to join him. She swam out past him and then he caught up with her. She grabbed on to the base of his tail and he powerfully swam back to shore towing her behind him. They kept doing this again and again. It was so much fun.

When they were tired enough, they went back to their
blanket, had another drink, and laid down to rest for
a while. This was the best day they had had in a very
long time. No babies, no puppies, just the two friends
and their mothers. What could be better?!

When they got home, they were very happy to see their families. Kermit let Fozzie Bear jump on him and lick him. He even shared some of his dinner, which was a rare occurrence. Kermit realized that having a new puppy wasn't so bad after all. His mommy loved them both equally, and having a bigger family now would be a lot of fun.

Jenna felt the same way, but she didn't share her food with her baby sister. Instead, she let the baby crawl all over her as they both rolled around on the floor, laughing together.

Kermit and Jenna slept very well that night and dreamed about their fun day at the beach.

Having a new puppy or a new baby wasn't so bad after all, as long as they got some fun time with their mommies.

Left to Right: Bonnie Giacovelli, Kermit the Newf, Fozzie Bear, Molly Tischler

Molly Tischler is Bonnie's mother. Upon retiring from a career as a financial advisor, she decided to pursue her lifelong passion for writing. What better subject could there be than her real life adventures with Kermit the Newf. She lives in Juno Beach, Florida, with her husband, Stephen.

Bonnie Giacovelli is a graduate of The College of the Atlantic, where she earned a Bachelor's degree in Human Ecology with a major in Zoology. She was diagnosed with Multiple Sclerosis more than twenty years ago. She is visually impaired and has balance issues. She trains her own service dogs to accommodate her needs. Kermit is her third service dog. She lives in Jupiter, Florida, with her husband, Lenny, and her other dogs and cats.

Kermit is a 10 ½-year-old Newfoundland dog, born and raised in Florida. He is a service dog, therapy dog, draft dog, model, and actor. He has been nominated three years in row for the AKC Humane Fund's ACE award, Achievement in Canine Excellence, in the therapy dog category. In 2013, he won Honorable Mention. He has done TV commercials, print ads, and corporate meet and greets. He has been in show business since he was eleven months old and has more than two dozen jobs to his credit. He enjoys competing in obedience, rally obedience, and conformation showing. He is also training to do water rescue. He is kind, gentle, sweet, and very intelligent. He loves people, especially children.

Fozzie Bear is 6 years old. He is Kermit's nephew. He is also a service dog and therapy dog. Just like his namesake, Fozzie Bear is sweet, funny, gentle, kind, smart, and occasionally a worrier. He loves playing in his pool and being with people.

Amy Bolin is living her childhood dream of drawing, painting, and sculpting dogs and cats for a living. She lives in Northern Michigan with her husband Troy, three sons, Jesse, Nile, and Gene, a big cat named Princess, a kitten called Ninja, and a lab-greyhound mix named Aiya.